The boxing champion

Story by Roch Carrier

Illustrations by Sheldon Cohen

Translated from the original French
by Sheila Fischman

BIENVENUE
à
STE. JUSTINE, QUÉ.
POP. 1200

Tundra Books

By April I knew it would happen again.

The rink was becoming soft. Our skate blades sank into the ice. The girls laughed when they saw us floundering around. The snow was gray. It was spring.

The street was a canal filled with water. Our ice forts were melting like cheese. Our snowmen were collapsing like fat drunken men.

The girls liked spring. They dreamed about the flowers they would soon be gathering in the grass. They strutted around in their coats and bright-colored berets.

The cows were waiting for our rink to turn into a pasture again.

The boys hated spring. There was nothing to do. Except school — and boxing…

The world champion was Joe Louis, the "Brown Bomber." His big swollen face often appeared in the newspaper. I didn't like the sport enough to put his picture on my bedroom wall next to one of Maurice Richard, the famous Number 9 of the Canadiens, our favorite hockey team.

And so when the rink was nothing but a big puddle, there we were in the Côtés' summer kitchen.

There were twelve Côté children, perhaps
thirteen. When the weather turned warm, the
family emigrated from the winter kitchen to the
summer kitchen, which was roomier, airier
and brighter. In the spring it was a big empty
space.

One of the Côtés had borrowed a piece of chalk
from school. He drew a big square on the
wooden floor. That was the ring. Another Côté
struck a big nail against a bottle. The bell!
And then two pugilists tore each other apart.
I applauded as hard as the others, but I
hated boxing.

I always did my best to be the last to climb into
the ring. My adversary would face me, skipping
and threatening me with his big fists. I danced
about, head down, I rolled my gloves. Wham!
I picked myself up on my rear end and my
nose was bleeding. The match had lasted as
long as a single punch. It wasn't me who
administered it.

Some of the girls at school used to come
to our fights. If one of the Côtés was hit, they
would coo. When I walked out of the ring,
stunned, my face bleeding, they didn't even see
me. I tried hard to bleed as much as possible.
They hadn't the slightest interest in me. Yet
deep down I knew I was a champion.

My friends were the sons of farmers, truckdrivers or loggers. Since their earliest childhood they had been doing the work of men. My nose knew that they punched like men.

Their bodies were stocky. They had broad shoulders and short arms and bowlegs. They were as tough as the wood of a maple. They wolfed down pork and pea soup. I should have fled, but I didn't want to be alone so I followed my friends.

My mother lit into me.

"Why on earth," she asked, "did you have to get mixed up with boxing again?"

And that was how things happened in the spring, in my village.

I had my tenth birthday, and then, the next winter, an ad in the newspaper drew my attention. "I'll make you a world champion," said a man with muscles like the Greek statues that illustrated our dictionaries. "In 33 days I became a champion who will represent Canada at the Olympic Games. Be like me. Send me five dollars and I'll reveal my secret."

Exactly what I needed! Along with a letter that didn't have a single mistake, I sent five one-dollar bills to the address mentioned. That same week I received a reply from the *Miracle Muscle Center*: "I can tell that you're the stuff of champions. Unfortunately, you must abandon hope unless you train with my very excellent 'Miracle Muscle Exercisers', as well as my 'Miracle Muscle Barbells'. To obtain them just send thirty dollars to the *Miracle Muscle Center*." I had thirty-two dollars in the bank.

My mother didn't want me to spend all my savings. She thought bank interest was as important as my muscles. Finally I told her:

"*Maman*, do you want your boy to have skinny little arms like a girl?"

She looked at me and said:

"If you don't have enough money, Roch, I'll give you a couple of dollars."

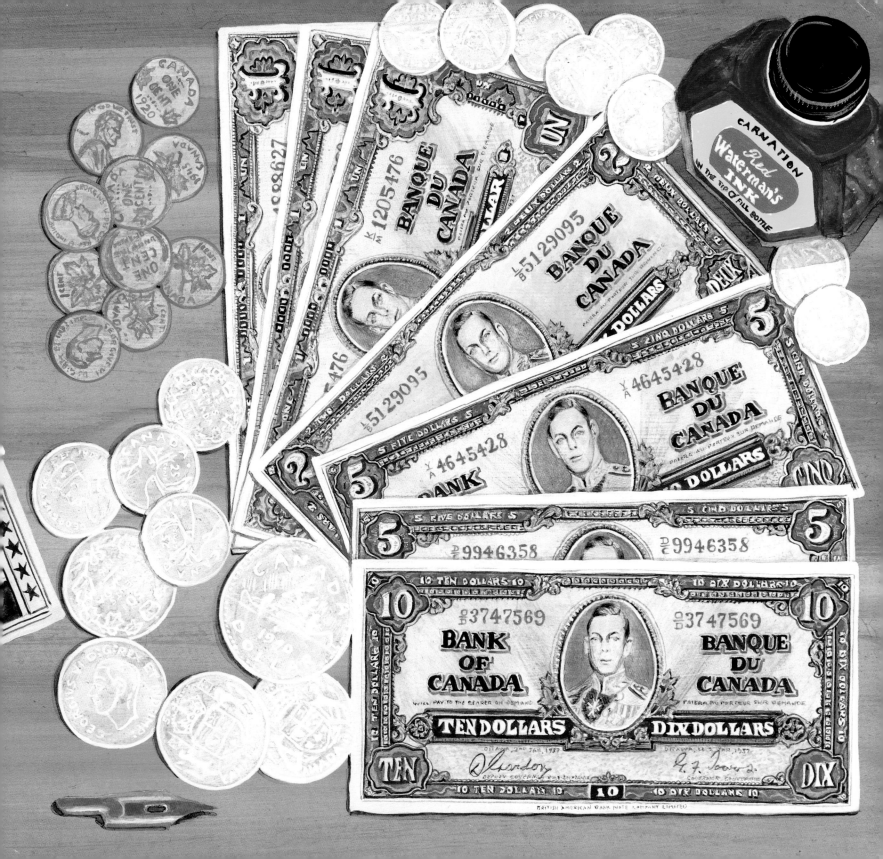

Soon I received my champion's arsenal. To surprise the Côtés, I must keep my strategy a total secret. First I obtained my sister's silence. That was easy. If she said one word about my training, I threatened to put a mouse in her bed. As for my brothers, if they kept my secret I promised them I wouldn't tell our mother that they got sick from smoking our grandfather's pipe.

Deep in my heart I knew I was a champion. Unfortunately, I'd never been able to prove it.

Secretly, I set to work. When I got up in the morning, instead of my prayers I repeated one hundred times: "I'm a champion."

I ran to school, chanting: "I'm a champion! I'm a champion!" During classes, I wrote over and over and over: "I'm a champion." According to my *Miracle Muscle Guide*, this was motivational auto-suggestion.

After school, when my homework was finally done, I raced to my exercisers. Fifty times, I spread my arms to pull open a single spring. Then I added a second one and struggled till I was exhausted. Sweating breathlessly, I whispered: "I'm a champion."

After supper I raced up to my room. To develop my calves I took the stairs three at a time.

"Roch!" exclaimed my mother. "Do you have to tear the house apart?"

I splashed some soapy water on my muzzle and launched into round one of my boxing match. It wasn't the biggest Côté boy, but I punched away. He was tough. I punched again: his nose, his ear, chin, belly, plexus, jaw.

Finally, I threw the definitive hook that would slam the biggest Côté to the floor. I trod on his earthly remains and got back into bed, triumphant. I lay there motionless and listened to the music of my muscles, which were developing as predicted in the *Miracle Muscle Guide*.

On other days, I took up my Miracle Muscle barbells. My hands were blistered. My shoulders creaked like rusty hinges. Instead of removing discs to lighten the load, I added more. My backbone cracked. My dorsal muscles burned like fire. I pulled. The flesh of my arms seemed to tear. My chest seemed to be descending into my stomach.

One day I would conquer adversaries far superior to the Côtés. I'd become the first French-Canadian boxing champion in the world! I was a champion. I knew it deep in my heart.

In the mirror I gazed at my biceps. They contained as much power as a cannon. My fists were as hard as cannonballs. My chest was as solid as the foundations of the church.

When I went to school I piled sweater upon sweater to disguise my new athlete's body. I had so many muscles now, it was almost impossible to hide them. That would be a surprise for the Côtés!

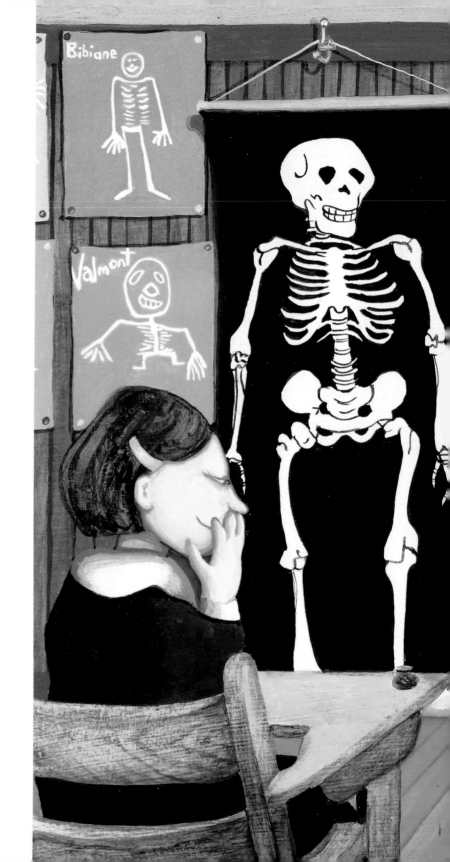

Now the winter was not so cold. I felt hot under my layers of sweaters. Water dripped from the icicles that hung from the roof. The rink was getting softer. It was spring!

Boxing season was starting up again. The boys and a few of the girls were in the Côtés' summer kitchen. We pushed back the table. Against the wall we piled skis, ski-poles, skates, snowshoes. Carefully, the oldest Côté traced the official limits of the ring in chalk.

"Who wants to fight?" asked the youngest Côté, leaping into the center.

"Get ready!" I cried.

Solemnly, I peeled off all my sweaters to show off my new muscles. My heart was pounding.

The youngest Côté burst out laughing.

"Where'd the plucked chicken come from? There isn't even enough for a sandwich."

A champion doesn't lose his head if he's insulted.

"Côté," I threatened between clenched teeth, "you'd better concentrate."

The bell rang. I attacked like a champion.

When I opened my eyes again I realized that I was stretched out in the ring. My nose was bleeding.

A young girl smiled at me and tossed me some wildflowers.

She was the prettiest girl in the whole class.

I'd never dared to talk to her.

What a wonderful spring it was!

© 1991 Roch Carrier: text
© 1991 Sheldon Cohen: illustration
© 1991 Sheila Fischman: translation

ISBN 0-88776-249-2 hardcover 10 9 8 7 6 5 4 3 2 1
ISBN 0-88776-257-3 softcover 10 9 8 7 6 5 4 3 2 1

Library of Congress Catalog Card Number: 90-70133

Also available in the original French edition, *Un champion*.
ISBN 0-88776-250-6 hardcover, ISBN 0-88776-258-1 softcover

Published in Canada by Tundra Books, Montreal, Quebec H3G 1R4

Published in the United States by Tundra Books of Northern New York, Plattsburgh, NY 12901

Distributed in the United Kingdom by Ragged Bears Ltd., Andover, Hampshire SP11 9HX
Distributed in France by Le Colporteur Diffusion, 84100 Orange

Canadian Cataloging in Publication Data

Carrier, Roch, 1937-
[Un champion. English]
    The Boxing Champion

Translation of: Un champion.
ISBN 0-88776-249-2

    I. Cohen, Sheldon, 1949-   . II. Title. III. Title: Un champion. English.

PS8505.A77C3913 1991   jC843'.54   C90-090155-1
PZ7.C37Bo 1991

Printed in Hong Kong by South China Printing Co. (1988) Ltd.

The author would like to dedicate this story to a little boy named Ariel.

The illustrator wishes to dedicate his work in this book to his son Matthew.

The translator dedicates her work in this book to Jake Wilson.